"It's moving straight towards Earth!" he said. "That comet is on a direct collision course with us!"

The General looked at him. "How long until impact?"

"Only four Earth hours, General."

The General stood up. "Order X-Bomber to take off and destroy that comet," he said sharply. "We have no time to waste. Meanwhile, sound the Red Alert."

"A comet on a direct collision course with Earth?" said Barry Hercules, as X-Bomber made its way across the dark expanse of sky.

"Yeah," said Shiro, glancing over at Lamia as she stood beside the menacing figure of Kirara. "Sounds a little fishy to me."

"Do you think it's a trap?" asked Lamia in her soft voice. "Or a trick by the Imperial Alliance?"

Shiro shrugged. "I don't know. But we'll have to be careful — and fast too. PPA, how far are we now from that comet?"

"Do you mean in distance or time?" the android asked pedantically. "I would say that it —"

"In time, you tin can," said Hercules impatiently. "We have only four earth hours to destroy this thing!"

"Less than that now," said PPA smugly. "In fact, you have only three hours and forty minutes — in earth time, of course."

"So how much time do we have before the comet is in range?" demanded Shiro.

"I would say about thirty minutes and seventeen seconds," said the android. "Approximately, that is; if you want a more accurate estimate, it will take a moment."

"That'll do, thanks," said Shiro wearily. "Increase speed, Barry. We haven't much time."

"You're telling me," remarked Barry. "Just what are we going to do to destroy this comet? Any ideas, Shiro?"

"We'll wait and see what we're up against when we get within range of it," said Shiro, "but there's no harm in checking all our weapons in the meantime."

The comet came into view.

"Wow!" said John Lee. "That's one large comet!"

It was indeed. The head of the comet roared on towards Earth, glowing with a brilliant white light, its aura swirling about it. The trail of gases swept along behind it, cutting a thick swathe of brilliance through the darkness of space.

"Well?" said Barry Hercules. "What does anyone suggest?"

Lamia was looking puzzled. "Shiro," she began hesitantly. Immediately the crew turned to her. "Doesn't the head of the comet look a little — well, solid — to you?"

Shiro looked out at the comet.

"I see what you mean," he said thoughtfully. "Yes, that doesn't seem like an ordinary comet to me. Barry, what's your opinion?"

Shiro in a puzzled voice. "She seems to be heading away from us. That's odd. Why won't she fight?"

"She's up to something," said Barry Hercules. "Makara doesn't turn her back on a fight unless she has a good reason."

Meanwhile, on board the battle cruiser, Makara was laughing to herself. "Good! The fools have left Earth and come out to investigate my comet! Now for the second part of my plan! Orion, release the catalyst!"

"But what about our own Imperial Fighters, commander? They are still out there."

"Are you daring to question an order?" demanded Makara icily.

"No, commander. But —"

"Star Fleet will be annihilated," said Makara. "If that is at the cost of one or two Imperial Fighters, so be it. They would be more than willing to sacrifice themselves for the sake of the glorious victory of the Imperial Alliance. Release the catalyst!"

"By your divine command," said Orion tremulously. "Release the catalyst!"

"There goes another," chortled John Lee, as another Imperial Fighter exploded in a myriad of stars.

"And only two to go," said Barry Hercules. "Yep! There goes another one! Who got that?"

"Not me," said Shiro. "John?"

"Nope."

"Funny," said Barry Hercules, in a puzzled voice.

"Cease fire a moment," said Shiro impulsively.

"Why?" asked John Lee.

"Just watch," said Shiro, "I think that fighter just blew up in mid-air."

The three of them watched as the remaining fighter swooped past them and veered off after the battle cruiser. Moments later it had reached the swirling cloud of gas. As it touched the gas, there was a flash, and the fighter vanished in a halo of sparks. Then there was nothing left but the gas, and some sinister-looking debris.

Barry Hercules opened his mouth to reply, but at that moment John Lee gave a cry.

"Look! That certainly isn't a genuine comet!"

The gases around the head of the object had parted slightly, perhaps blown about by the disturbance caused by X-Bomber. Beneath them, Shiro and Barry could see the dark gleam of metal and an all too familiar insignia.

"It's Makara's battle cruiser!" said Lamia. "And look! Imperial Fighters!"

"Makara must have realised that we'd spotted her little ruse," said Shiro grimly. "She'd hardly order the launch of those tin mosquitoes otherwise."

Quickly he set X-Bomber on to automatic, and the three pilots rushed to their machine-guns. As the insect-like enemy craft swooped towards them, the guns went off with bursts of light and three of the fighters exploded into nothing.

"Got 'em!" chuckled John Lee.

"Makara's taken fright," said

"Whew!" whistled Barry. "It just burned up."

"It's the gas," said Shiro. "I've seen something like it before. It simply burns up everything it touches — just on contact."

"Nasty stuff," put in John Lee.

"And it's still headed towards Earth," added Barry.

"You're right," said Shiro. "We have to do something. That amount of gas could destroy the Earth! That's really vicious stuff!"

"Vicious ain't the word," said John Lee. Nobody contradicted him.

General Kyle sat down heavily. The message from X-Bomber had not been good. What could he do now? Evacuate the Earth base altogether? Or put up defensive shields against a gas that would just burn them up on contact?

Nothing he could think of seemed practical. He had never in his long experience come across anything like this gas before. Who else was likely to have done so?

"Send for Doctor Benn," he ordered quickly. "I think we had better start evacuation procedure as soon as possible too."

Doctor Benn was roused and made his way to the General. "What is it?" he asked urgently. "What's the trouble?"

"X-Bomber reports a very large amount of gas floating towards Earth," said the General. "This gas is like nothing I have ever come across before. It burns objects to nothing, merely on contact. There is enough of it, according to Space Pilot Hagen, to destroy the Earth."

"Oh no!" exclaimed the Doctor in a horrified whisper. "And X-Bomber is still up there with it?"

"Awaiting your advice or instructions, Doctor. Have you ever dealt with this sort of thing before?"

The Doctor nodded slowly. "Once, some time ago. It was when I was a young research student on Mars, with Professor Hagen, Shiro's father. This gas was created by accident in the laboratories, but its lethal properties were not discovered until it came into contact with one of Professor Hagen's own discoveries — a substance which acts as a catalyst on this gas, and makes it deadly. I wish I knew where the Imperial Alliance found the formula for this gas and its catalyst."

"Is there a neutralising agent for this gas?" asked the General.

Doctor Benn shook his head. "I'm afraid not. It would take days

to discover one, and we haven't time for that. Let me think for a moment."

He rested his chin in his hands and closed his eyes. The General paced up and down, his hands clasped behind his back, listening to the well ordered bustle of the evacuation. For some time the Doctor sat thinking. The cloud of gas on the star screen was getting steadily closer, the shape of X-Bomber tracking it closely — yet not too closely.

Finally Doctor Benn opened his eyes. "General," he said, "I have the solution. But it will take every ship you have to do it."

"Every ship?" echoed the General. "And you guarantee that this will work; because if it doesn't, we will all be dead."

"I can give no guarantee," said Doctor Benn gravely. "I can only suggest this idea. It is up to the pilots of the space craft to carry the mission out successfully."

"What is your plan?" asked the General.

"I don't believe it," said Shiro flatly.

"Shiro, what is happening?" asked Lamia. Beside her, Kirara growled and muttered. "How are we to destroy this gas?"

Shiro looked across at Barry Hercules and John Lee, then back at Lamia. "You'll never believe this," he said, "but we have been ordered to wait for other craft from Earth base, and then to blow it away."

"*Blow* it?" said Hercules, incredulously. "Has someone finally flipped down there? How do we blow it away?"

"Simple," said John Lee. "We just lean out and do a lot of deep breathing. Isn't that right, Shiro?"

"Not exactly," said Shiro, smiling. "What we're supposed to do is to throw all engines into reverse, and blow it away like that."

"That's all very well," said Barry Hercules. "But what about the rest of the solar system? We can't allow all that gas to float about unchecked, surely? What about the other planets? All those people? I wouldn't wish that gas on anyone — even Makara."

"I would — on Makara," said John Lee, grimly. "She wished it on us, remember?"

"Well, we have to remember that we're only here to carry out orders," said Shiro. "Although I agree with Barry that it's wrong to let that stuff float around in space, burning things up all the time."

"So what do we do now?" asked Lamia softly. "Do we follow our orders or query them?"

Shiro smiled at her. "We follow them, of course," he said. "But we also point out to Headquarters what they may have overlooked."

He flicked a switch and opened

screen. "I think . . . they are coming to the aid of X-Bomber."

"I can see that, imbecile," snapped Makara. "But to aid it in doing what? What do they think they can do against that gas? There is no antidote, no neutraliser for it. Our scientists made sure of that when two of their number died in its manufacture. What do the idiots think they can do?"

"X-Bomber is turning round," remarked Orion, hesitantly.

"Why?" demanded Makara. "Why is it turning? Is it retreating? Is General Kyle going to evacuate the Earth at last? If so, we shall have them right where we have always wanted them!"

"We're still being watched," said John Lee. "That Makara is still hovering about, Shiro."

"I know," said Shiro, grinning. "Shall we give her a fright?"

He turned on the engines, increasing their power. A blast of air shot out of the ship and blew a hole in the boundary of the gas. On the other side of it, a bulge of

communications with Earth base.

"General Kyle from Shiro Hagen. Come in, please."

The General's grave face appeared on the screen. "Kyle here."

"General. This scheme for blowing away the gas — what about the rest of the solar system? The gas'll just float about burning up all it touches! We can't let that happen!"

Doctor Benn appeared next to the General. "Shiro, that won't happen. I am working on a neutraliser for the gas, but we have no time to question things now. By my calculations, the gas will not reach another planet for three earth days — if you perform your orders satisfactorily. That may give me time to deal with the problem, and there will have been no loss of life."

Lamia spoke up. "Have you the

necessary assistance, Doctor?"

The Doctor smiled. "Yes, my dear. Adequate, but never as helpful as you are. Don't worry."

"How long will it take those ships to reach us?" asked Shiro. "Will they get here in time?"

"I think so," said General Kyle. "You had better start your own manoeuvres as soon as possible."

"Right," said Shiro.

He switched off the screen and snapped out a couple of brisk orders. Hercules and Lee leapt to attention, and the giant ship began slowly to turn itself about.

Makara watched what was going on. "What are they doing?" she demanded of Orion. "What is happening here? They cannot possibly escape from my gas field. And what are all these other ships doing?"

Orion looked at the scanner

the stuff appeared, pushing its way towards the battle cruiser.

"Well," said Barry Hercules, "it seems to push that stuff about all right. The question is, how long will it be before the rest of those ships arrive from Earth to help us?"

"Docter Benn said it would be in time," said Lamia. "I'm sure we can trust him to be accurate, Barry."

The pilot smiled. "Yes, Lamia, I know we can — but can we trust Makara not to put any obstacle in their way?"

"Obstacle?"

Barry looked at Shiro gravely. "Yes, obstacle. Like herself, with that battle cruiser of hers, or the Imperial Fighters she must still have on board the cruiser."

"I hadn't thought of that," said Lamia with a worried tone in her voice. "Do you think she might do that?"

"Knowing Makara," said Shiro, "I think it's very likely."

Doctor Benn bent over a sheet of calculations. If he was right, then Star Fleet stood every chance of blowing away that gas long enough for him to work out

the formula for a neutraliser.

But were his calculations correct? He knew he had been overworking and was very tired — and although the help he was receiving was valuable, it did not have the bright brainwork that Lamia brought to his laboratories.

He sighed. It would be a lot easier if he could only remember where he had stored the formula for the gas made by Professor Hagen. He knew the computer's recent memory banks by heart — but the older ones were a problem. Lamia would know — she had made it her business to catalogue every single item in the computer, and her extraordinary memory was invaluable.

Meanwhile, General Kyle stood in the control room at Earth base headquarters. He was worried — very worried. Only a few minutes could make so much difference to this mission — in fact they could mean the end of Earth, if something went wrong, and with all the craft out in space there was no chance of quick evacuation should something go wrong.

He hoped that Makara would have vanished by now — back to wherever it was she lurked when she wasn't spearheading attacks on the defence forces he commanded. But he knew that was a vain hope. She would be there as usual, waiting like a spider for the flies to drop into her net.

"Are those ships within range?" asked Makara, watching the screen intently. Orion paused to check.

"They are, commander."

"Good. Now, you will wait to attack until I give the order. When I do, I want every weapon possible trained on those relief craft out there, but not on X-Bomber. Do you understand?"

"Not on X-Bomber?" queried Orion.

"That is what I said. I want that ship intact, so that the Imperial Alliance may learn from those tricks it performs. But the smaller craft, we may destroy those at our leisure."

"By your divine command," said Orion.

Makara paused, watching the screen. The ships grew nearer and nearer, apparently unaware that they were being watched, concentrating on the dense cloud of gas.

"Now, attack!" cried Makara shrilly, and the guns of the battle cruiser began to blast at the small craft.

"Oh no!" whispered Shiro, as several of the relief ships blew up. "I knew she would do that! Why didn't I warn them sooner?"

"You did all you could," said Hercules grimly. "You warned them. You warned General Kyle. The question now is how do we get rid of this gas? We haven't enough power to blow it away."

"Shall I contact Doctor Benn?" asked Lamia.

"No," said Shiro impulsively. "No, we will deal with this ourselves. We'll blast the thing away. Barry, prepare the X-Impulse."

PPA floated past his head. "You know you can only use the X-Impulse once," it warned happily.

"I know, PPA," said Shiro. "I don't intend to make any mistakes though. I just hope it works."

"I don't see why it should," said Barry Hercules. "Firing at gas doesn't make it disappear."

"No," said Lamia thoughtfully, "but the X-Impulse gives off tremendous heat, and that might do something to the gas. I can remember going through the computer banks, and discovering something about this gas. If only I could remember what it was. I know exactly where it is, too."

"Well, we haven't time to check, I'm afraid," said Shiro. "This gas has got to be eliminated now, before millions die. Fire the Impulse, Barry."

"There she goes!" said Barry, and the four wings of the Bomber lit up with a brilliant light, their power concentrated into one huge beam.

"It is that laser thing again!" shrieked Makara on the battle cruiser. "Retreat! We will be

damaged if that comes within reach of us!"

But the beam did not reach them. It fell directly on to the cloud of gas, and seemed to be absorbed by it. Then, there was a strange sight to be seen . . .

"Look at that!" breathed Barry Hercules in amazement.

"A great big flying iceberg!" chuckled John Lee.

"And it's been pushed in the direction of the battle cruiser," added Shiro. "I bet that's given Makara a nasty fright!"

The gas had solidified and now floated in the dark expanse of space like a huge lump of ice. It seemed to glow, as if the power of the laser beam had been caught inside it and trapped. Beyond it, the battle cruiser was retreating fast, loath to remain and watch the glowing iceberg following it.

"Well, you know what they say," said John Lee, grinning. "A thing of beauty is a joy for ever. And if that thing keeps right on Makara's tail, it'll give *me* some joy, I can tell you!"

Lamia smiled. "It won't, John. Sooner or later, it will just fade away as it comes into contact with other atmospheres. But in the meantime, it will just drift aimlessly in the wake of the battle cruiser."

"I can think of better places to

be," said Shiro, smiling. "In the meantime, shall we return to Earth?"

"That would be a good idea," said John Lee, "except that I wanted to watch this a while longer."

"Oh, come on," said Barry Hercules, "you know how much the iceberg is going to worry Makara, without having to watch it. Besides, Lamia's itching to get back to her computers, aren't you, Lamia?"

He took a couple of steps towards her. Immediately, Kirara jumped in front of the girl, eyes flashing fiercely, hairy face snarling a threat.

"Okay," said Barry warily. "I know when I'm not welcome. Let's go home!"

ST★R PROBE

How much do you know about the Solar System, where so much of the action in *Star Fleet* takes place? This is a quiz designed for you by Shiro Hagen and the rest of the Star Fleet crew, to see if you measure up to their high standards!
How many answers can you get right?

1. In what year was the first satellite — the USSR Sputnik — launched?

2. In 1962 an American became the first human to orbit the earth. What was his name?

3. What was the V-2? What powered it?

4. What is the largest planet in the Solar System?

5. What three species of animals have travelled in space?

6. Who was the first woman to travel in space?

7. What is the nearest star to earth?

8. Which constellation is sometimes called the Big Dipper?

9. Which planet is named after the Roman god of war?

10. Which is the farthest planet from the sun?

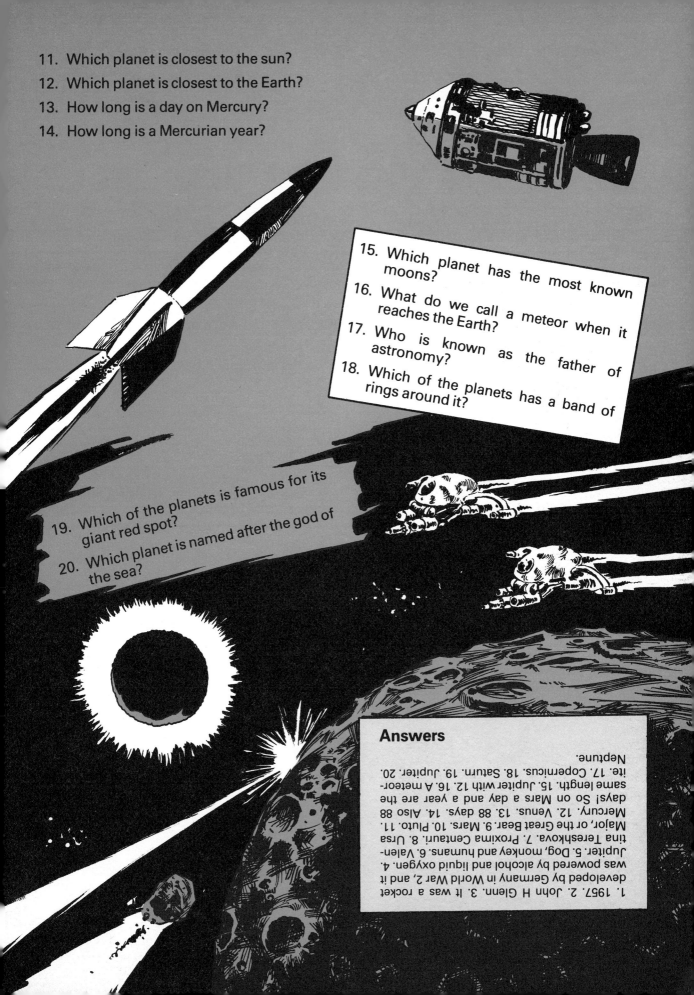

11. Which planet is closest to the sun?

12. Which planet is closest to the Earth?

13. How long is a day on Mercury?

14. How long is a Mercurian year?

15. Which planet has the most known moons?

16. What do we call a meteor when it reaches the Earth?

17. Who is known as the father of astronomy?

18. Which of the planets has a band of rings around it?

19. Which of the planets is famous for its giant red spot?

20. Which planet is named after the god of the sea?

Answers

1. 1957. 2. John H Glenn. 3. It was a rocket developed by Germany in World War 2, and it was powered by alcohol and liquid oxygen. 4. Jupiter. 5. Dog, monkey and humans. 6. Valentina Tereshkova. 7. Proxima Centauri. 8. Ursa Major, or the Great Bear. 9. Mars. 10. Pluto. 11. Mercury. 12. Venus. 13. 88 days. 14. Also 88 days! So on Mars a day and a year are the same length. 15. Jupiter with 12. 16. A meteorite. 17. Copernicus. 18. Saturn. 19. Jupiter. 20. Neptune.

Death in the
DOOMSDAY ZOO

Once the raiding party of Alliance Imperial Fighters had been driven off and the safety of the Star Fleet supply ships had been assured, Doctor Benn went to work checking the damage to X-Bomber.

"Shiro?"

Shiro checked the readings on his control console.

"Left X-Machine Gun inoperative," he reported.

"Copy, Shiro," said Doctor Benn. "Hercules?"

"Retro engines on Jumbody took a direct hit," said Barry Hercules ruefully.

"John Lee?" asked Doctor Benn. John Lee didn't answer.

"John Lee?" repeated Doctor Benn. "Do you copy?"

"I copy, Doctor Benn," said John Lee, peering intently at the screen in front of him, "but you'd better see this for yourself."

"What is it?" asked Doctor Benn, joining John Lee at his post.

"These readings," said John Lee, "they would seem to indicate a large number of humanoid life forms in this quadrant of space."

"That's impossible!" said Doctor Benn. "The only humanoids who could exist in this quadrant were the Straglidods, and they were all wiped out in the war."

"Can you be certain of that?" asked Lamia.

Doctor Benn nodded sombrely. "Have you ever seen what a Megabeam Particle Cannon does to a planet?" he asked. "Left in orbit it can reduce the surface to a lifeless cloud of dust and steam within a week."

"But that's another thing," said John Lee. "Our records show that there are only six planets in this particular solar system."

"And?"

"And our sensors say there are seven."

"The sensors must have been damaged in the fighting," said Shiro.

"Possibly," said Doctor Benn. "I think one of us had better go out and check the probes on the hull."

"I'll do it," volunteered Shiro.

"No," said Hercules. "I'll go. We'll need you here in case those bully-boy Alliance thugs show up again." He began suiting up for the spacewalk. "And besides," he added, checking the controls on his jet pack, "when it comes to spacewalking — you're still in the crawling stage."

Shiro let the good-natured insult pass.

"Okay, Hercules," he said, "get out there and do your stuff."

Barry Hercules climbed through the airlock and, using short bursts from his jet pack to correct his position, made his way along the hull of X-Bomber, checking all the sensors and probes he could find.

"Any damage?" asked Doctor Benn over the communicator.

"Negative," replied Hercules. "I'm going to check the rear sector now."

"Hold on a minute," interrupted John Lee urgently, "I've got something — Holy stars! Get back inside, Hercules, there's a meteor pack coming in fast!"

"What's the E.T.A.?" asked Hercules calmly.

"Estimated Time of Arrival . . . twenty-eight seconds!" shrilled PPA.

"Prepare for evasive action," ordered Doctor Benn.

"Step on it, Hercules!" said Shiro.

"Seventeen seconds," piped PPA, "sixteen . . . fifteen . . ."

"I'm not going to make it, Shiro," said Hercules. "Get X-Bomber out of here!"

"No!" shouted Lamia.

"Nine . . . eight . . . seven . . ." droned PPA.

Shiro hesitated over the controls.

"Do as I say!" shouted Hercules angrily. "X-Bomber must be saved! I'll take my chances with the meteors."

"But the blast from the engines —" began Shiro, helplessly.

"Four . . . three . . . two . . ."

"Do as Hercules says, Shiro," ordered Doctor Benn.

Lamia held her hand to her mouth.

Shiro punched the controls and X-Bomber leapt into life as the fiery hail of red hot rocks rained down upon them.

"Good luck," whispered Lamia, almost to herself.

As X-Bomber moved out of danger, Barry Hercules hit the controls on his jet pack and headed into the meteorite pack at full power. He was determined that if he had to die he would meet death head on. As the storm of

flaming space debris raged around him, he imagined he saw, in the eye of that same storm, a gigantic silver ball-bearing. And then his visor exploded in a white flash that turned slowly to red, and then black.

When Hercules came to he felt like he'd been given the once over by a Samallian Dragoid. His head throbbed, his whole body ached and his lungs burned with every breath he took. He also found he couldn't move.

"Another fine specimen, I see," said a voice.

Hercules opened his eyes and saw an Alliance guard standing over him with an electric whip. He looked down at his body and saw that it was strapped to a table.

"Who are you?" he asked. "Where am I?"

"Don't ask questions!" snarled the guard, lashing out with the whip. Hercules felt a searing, stabbing pain where it hit home.

"You ought to be grateful we saved your life," sneered the guard, "but after a few years in our little homestead — somehow I don't think you will. Take him down to the cube!"

Hercules felt rough hands unfastening him and lifting him up. He was carried across the room and thrown head first into a round metal tube. He slid downwards for several minutes and came out with a bump in a tiny square room that already held three other prisoners. One of them, a green dwarf whose head was set in the middle of his chest, walked over and helped him to his feet.

"Sorry about the welcome," he said. "My name's Harg."

"Hi, Harg. Where am I?" asked Barry.

"You're on AAAPES — the Artificial Automated Alliance Planetoid (Experimental Sector). At least that's what the guards call it. We call it the Doomsday Zoo."

"Why's that?" asked Barry Hercules.

"Because this place is where the Alliance tests all its weapons — on us. Bacteriological weapons, viral weapons, particle beams — right down to good old electric whips."

"Yes," said Hercules, fingering the welt caused by the guard's whip, "I've already had a taste of the last one."

Harg introduced Hercules to his cube-mates. There was B, a skinny reptilian from Alpha Millenni, and Uncular, a space nomad who looked like a giant ball of wool. Harg could speak to them both fluently in their own language.

"Any questions?" asked Harg, when he'd finished the introductions.

"Just one," said Hercules.

"What's that?"

"When do we get out of here?"

Harg smiled and shook Hercules' hand. "I was hoping you'd say that."

The wall of the cube slid upwards and a guard led them down a long corridor.

"We're on body duty today," explained Harg. "We pick up all the bodies and send them up the anti-gravity chute to the laboratories."

Hercules grimaced. His mind was working fast on a way out of the evil prison.

"If we could get to the laboratories," he whispered to Harg, "could we get hold of any weapons?"

"Stop talking!" shouted the guard, prodding Hercules with a stun-stick. "Get to work!"

Hercules, Harg, B, and Uncular went about their grisly task, whispering among themselves

whenever they could. By the time the first batch had been sent floating up the chute, they had agreed on their plan — when the guards changed they would jump them and make their way up to the laboratories in the anti-gravity chute.

"I thought I told you to stop talking!" The guard lashed B across his back.

"For your insolence you will be used as an amusement for our honoured guest — Commander Makara!"

Hercules stiffened at the mention of Makara's name. If she were to recognise him . . . he kept his head down as the guard handed B over to a passing patrol.

When B returned there were large green stripes across his back and light blue tears were falling from his eyes. The guard laughed pitilessly.

"Did you have some fun?" he asked, raising his whip. "Maybe you'd like a little more?"

As the whip snaked out, Barry Hercules leapt forward and grabbed it. Despite the burning pain he pulled as hard as he could, and as the guard tottered forward, Harg jumped in and felled him with a blow to the back of the neck.

"Well done," said Hercules. "Now, let's go!"

They took the guard's clothing and made ready to ride the anti-gravity chute as they had planned — B first, Uncular second, Barry third and Harg last. As B stepped forward Harg placed his hand on his shoulder and began talking quietly in a language Hercules couldn't understand.

Above the prisoners, Commander Makara was enjoying her visit. The idea of the Doomsday Zoo was one that appealed to her, as was the idea that the Operation Officer had put to her. How amus-

ing it would be to raise the hopes of Hercules and Harg, when all the time they had been set up by B and Uncular, two loyal Alliance plants.

"They'll be coming past this window here, Commander," said the Operations Officer, pointing to a screen in the anti-gravity chute. "They should make a pretty sight when we grill them alive with our microwave handguns."

"They should indeed," agreed Makara, accepting the pistol from the Operations Officer. A guard checked a gauge on the wall.

"They're coming!" he warned. "Don't forget to let the first two pass — they're very useful to us as spies."

Makara nodded as the first two bodies flew past the window and the guard pulled a lever.

"They're on hold!" said the Operations Officer. "Open fire!"

Makara and the officer pulled the triggers and the deadly rays went into action. It was only when the smoke cleared and they got a good glimpse of their victims that they realised they'd been fooled.

"But — but —" whined the Operations Officer, gazing at the charred, floating bodies of Uncular and B.

"You   imbecile!"   seethed

Makara. "They must have tumbled your plan! Send a squad up to the laboratories immediately!"

Inside the laboratories, Harg and Hercules had captured the technicians and were holding them at bay with laser scalpels. The fight had been a short one as the technicians had been ready to receive only spies or dead bodies — and Harg and Barry Hercules were very much alive.

"There's an emergency lifepod in the next bay," said one of the technicians. "Take it! Go! Only

please don't kill us!" He got to his knees and begged.

"You take the pod, Harg," said Hercules. "I'm going to stay here and blow this stinking prison out of existence!"

"You take it!" said Harg. "It's no use to me. They injected me weeks ago. I'll blow the Doomsday Zoo!"

"None of you will!" said the technician, getting off his knees. "The guards are in the corridor outside! Listen! It's too late!"

He was right. Hercules and Harg could hear the guards in the corridor between them and the lifepod.

"I guess this is it," said Hercules. "If we can't put an end to all this suffering by blowing the place up — at least we can go down fighting!"

"It would be an honour to die beside you," said Harg, fiddling with some switches on the laboratory communications computer. "But it may not be necessary after all."

"What do you mean?" asked Hercules.

"I can speak any language," explained Harg, "I can mimic any sound, any voice!"

"So?"

"So, listen." Harg pushed a red button and began speaking, his voice an exact replica of Commander Makara's. "Red Alert One! Red Alert One! This is Commander Makara speaking. All guards to report immediately to Green Bay Three. Repeat — all guards to Green Bay Three. All other orders are countermanded. Repeat —"

Harg winked at Hercules as they heard the guards in the corridor leaving.

"Now get out of here," said Harg. "I've got some work to do on this computer. Demolition work!"

Barry Hercules shook his hand, ran down the corridor to the lifepod and ejected into the blackness of space.

As he floated further and further from the Doomsday Zoo he saw the metal planetoid glow red. Hundreds of ships tried to escape the inevitable blast, abandoning their mothership like rats, but only a handful made it. Then the darkness of space erupted into a ball of white hot shrapnel and the Doomsday Zoo was no more.

The air in the lifepod was down to 30 per cent when X-Bomber hauled it aboard. The rough humour of the crew did little to conceal the joy they felt at finding their comrade again, alive and well.

"It would appear you've had quite an adventure," said Doctor Benn, eyeing the state of Hercules' uniform.

"Put it this way," replied Hercules, "it's the most tiring trip to the zoo that I've ever had!"

The X-Bomber — Who Can Beat It?

X-Bomber has five powerful weapons — and it needs them all in order to fight off the threat of the evil Imperial Alliance! So let's have a look at these weapons in more detail.

X-Impulse is the most powerful of the weapons, and is used only as a last resort, as it requires enormous amounts of energy to fire, and hence can only be used once at a time. The Impulse is an ultra beam thrown out by the four X-shaped wings of X-Bomber, and it is deadly.

Rather than use the Impulse, though, the crew of X-Bomber have four other weapons to use first against a hostile craft.

Firstly, there is the *Brest Cannon*, which is hidden in the main body of the Bomber. A very high-powered weapon, this cannon can cause great destruction to enemy craft. To fire it, X-Bomber's long nose must first be lifted, which also means that the weapon has the additional advantage of surprise.

Found on the tips of the four wings is the *Electro-Magnetic Cannon*, which emits extremely powerful electro-magnetic energy capable of causing extensive damage.

To the right, left and centre of X-Bomber are the *X-Machine Guns*, easily controlled weapons for dealing with smaller enemy craft. And finally, at the top of X-Bomber, is the *X-Electro Magnetic Gun*, which destroys enemy ships with a succession of deadly shots.

You have to agree that with weapons like these, and a crew like X-Bomber's, the Imperial Alliance doesn't stand a chance of achieving it's evil aims!

THE HUNT

There were four caves on the slope of the ridge and Makara's hunting creatures had already reached the first of them. Shiro, crouched in the highest of the caves, watched them go in. He had thought about dying before; part of his training as a Star Fleet pilot had required that he contemplate his own death in combat, but he had never pictured it like this, never thought that he would die like this, alone and stranded on a strange planet, hunted down by Makara and her pack of mutants. Even when he thought back to how it had started it hardly seemed possible.

It had started when a peaceful freighter had been blown up somewhere between Cassiopia and the Dog Star. By the time X-Bomber had arrived from patrolling an adjacent quadrant it was already too late for the freighter. All that was left of her were twisted shards of metal and the eerie sonar echoes of her captain's last stricken calls for help bouncing off the still, silent walls of space. They rang in the ears of X-Bomber's crew as they scanned the quadrant for signs of an attacker.

It had been Barry Hercules who had locked his scanner onto the faint phosphorescent trail of after-images that spacecraft leave behind when they are approaching hyperspeeds. From the shape of the images Shiro could tell the ship was large, maybe even the Gelmar Force's battle cruiser. With contact made, the crew of X-Bomber prepared for interception with the practised efficiency that their years of training and combat experience had instilled in them.

Shiro looked at the figures as the course computer printed them out. It was going to be close, maybe too close. He'd wanted to head the attacker off before it reached hyperspeed, but it looked now as if they were both going to reach the crossover point together. If they were travelling at quantum speeds they would collide. If they'd reached hyperspeeds then it wasn't so predictable. Whatever happened, it was going to get bumpy.

"Seven hundred miles and closing fast," Fatty Lee called out as he picked up the reading on his radar screens. "Six fifty, five hundred. Estimated time of impact seven seconds."

So they had lost the gamble, thought Shiro, they couldn't intercept the attacker. He glanced down at their speed. Already they were travelling too fast to use their lasers. It was just a matter of holding on now. Already he could feel that heaviness and density in his body that occurs in those moments before the crossover into hyperspace. He prayed it would come in time.

"Four twenty five, four hundred, three fifty, still closing."

"Visual contact established, it's Orion's Carrier all right."

"Two hundred and still closing. Encountering turbulence."

Shiro could see the Gelmar cruiser closing on them from the starboard quarter and could feel the shuddering in X-Bomber as the force fields from the two ships began to overlap. They could only wait now — wait, hope and watch what happened. The range between the two ships continued to close; less than a hundred miles, less than fifty, than twenty.

It's too late, thought Shiro, we've run out of space, we're going to collide, and he braced himself automatically against an impact that would destroy them all.

But then, suddenly, the nature of the space and light around them began to change, become fluid, to curl over on itself like a breaking wave as the points that it came from and everything it illuminated were fused together, and the two space ships were drawn into a dark spiralling vortex as both dematerialised in the milliseconds that preceded impact.

Shiro sat silent in his cave and remembered. Beneath him he could hear Makara's taunts and the weird snarls of her hunting creatures. He remembered how silent everything had been on X-Bomber. The silence had seemed to last for an eternity, an eternity in which X-Bomber's crew had realised that nothing was as it should be. The systems which should have been computing their point of re-entry into quantum space were functioning erratically. The scanners that should have recorded nothing in the timeless empty nowhere of hyperspace were transmitting readings which should not have been possible. And the impossible had not been only on the scanners, for beside Shiro, where Doctor Benn should have been standing, stood Makara, commander of the Gelmar Forces and chief confidant of the Imperial Master of the Alliance.

Shiro had blinked, looked out of the observation port, and again what he had seen made no sense. There was X-Bomber, and beside it the Gelmar Force's battle cruiser and beside that another X-Bomber, and beside that another cruiser, thousands upon thousands of the craft receding away from him until they were too distant for his eyes to focus upon.

"One of the riddles of hyperspace," he heard Makara say behind him, and he had felt her black claw upon his shoulder. Shiro felt his hand move almost automatically to the pistol at his belt but the claw grasped his arm. "Shoot me if you want, Hagen, but it would be a pointless gesture," hissed Makara. "In hyperspace there are an infinite number of Makaras just as there are an infinite number of Shiro Hagens. You could no more kill them than count them. Who do you think are aboard those ships you see out there, Hagen, except ourselves?"

"Then what's happened to Doctor Benn?"

"The same thing that has happened to all of us. Take a look around you at your crew." Shiro glanced around X-Bomber's cabin. Once again he was unable to understand what he saw. Lamia was there, but Kirara was missing, and beside John Lee, where Barry Hercules should have been, was Captain Orion.

"You still don't understand, do you, Hagen?" he heard Makara's sneering voice ask him. "Our ships have entered the infinity of hyperspace at the same point — we have occupied a spatial overlap which has turned one of the puzzles of infinity into a problematical reality. You will find your good Doctor Benn on some of those ships out there, sometimes as the commander of an Alliance craft crewed by Star Fleet, sometimes an X-Bomber crewed by Gelmar Forces. Sometimes, as in our own case, by an amalgam of both, while at other times the situation is exactly as it was before. The series is endless, Hagen, the possibilities infinite."

"Correction required," interrupted PPA. "The possibilities must range from the infinite down to zero. Therefore the possibilities are numbered. Simply because the number is an unknown does not mean . . ."

"You dare to interrupt me?" shrieked Makara angrily, and she brought down her sword on the tiny robot, her blows reducing it to a wreckage of smashed circuits and capacitors. Shiro reached for his pistol once again but once again Makara stopped him. "The gesture was pleasant but meaningless, Hagen. Remember that in infinity there are an infinite number of PPAs. However much I may wish otherwise I can destroy nothing in hyperspace. We are trapped here together, Shiro Hagen, though for you escape is more urgent. How long do you think the Thalian zone can survive the Imperial Master's attacks without X-Bomber to protect it?"

"And how fierce an attack can the Imperial Master launch without the Gelmar Force's battle-cruiser?"

Makara shrugged. "As you wish, Hagen. But remember, you are sworn to defend the power while I am sworn to acquire it. Which of us has more to lose?" Shiro made no reply and she continued. "You see? It is a risk that you cannot afford to take. That is why the price for my co-operation will cost you so high. If you agree to it then I shall be willing to help you."

"That depends," said Shiro.

"Very well. You must take X-Bomber back into quantum space. When this happens all other possibilities must reduce accordingly. All that will remain here in hyperspace then will be the cruiser and all the people who are not on X-Bomber. That is everyone except ourselves. They are the other half of the jigsaw. They will then be free to leave hyperspace themselves and the two ships will rendezvous at a meeting point I shall arrange — and there each of us shall transfer the other's unwelcome guests."

"And what's your price for this, Makara?"

"That when both ships depart, Hagen, you are left behind in a lifepod."

"But that's murder," said Fatty Lee.

Makara gave a cruel smile. "Not so, my fat friend, not so. Though the pod must be unarmed and without food supplies I am prepared to allow Hagen a day's supply of oxygen. Then he can spend all day thinking about what it will be like when it runs out."

"Shiro," said Lamia, "you mustn't do it."

"Oh but he must," said Makara, "and quickly! Remember, amongst that infinity of X-Bombers and cruisers there might be other Makaras who are planning to cross back into quantum space with enemy forces aboard, and they might not be so generous as I. Another Makara might kill anyone she has on board. It could be Lamia, or you, Lee, or your friend Hercules. It could even be the good Doctor Benn. And it won't just be taking place in the theoretical infinities of hyperspace like the damage I've done to that grotesque little talking ball. It'll be taking place in quantum space and time, my friends, in what's commonly known as the real world."

"He's right," Shiro had said bitterly, "I have no choice."

Shiro's memories were interrupted by the hideous creatures emerging from the lowest of the caves and scrambling across the smooth black boulders to the entrance of the second one.

Makara was calling out to him. "It's no use, Hagen. They have your scent. They have studied your ways beside the fire. They know you and you will die."

Not yet, thought Shiro grimly, as the creatures scrambled over one another into the second cave yelping, and once again he found his thoughts going back to the events that had brought him here.

Shiro and the crew of X-Bomber had given their word to Makara and they had kept it. After the two spacecraft had rendezvoused and their crews returned, Shiro had been cast adrift in an un-armed lifepod. As the two space-craft had disappeared in their different directions he had studied the Star Fleet charts he had brought with him and dis-covered that with careful use of the lifepod's small rocket system it might just be possible for him to reach Teltos.

Teltos was a small planet, about one quarter the size of the Earth, and in the years before the great devastation it had been a thriving place, mined for its metals and minerals. But now it was an empty desolate place, honeycombed with tunnels, and its ruined towns and cities were supposedly un-inhabited. Shiro had heard rumours that the place was still populated by mutated descend-ants of the original mining colonies, children of the great devastation, but no one knew for sure whether or not such stories were true. The place was marked as inhospitable on the Star Fleet chart, but where else was there for him to go?

Shiro had too little fuel to bring the lifepod in for a piloted landing. He'd simply gone into orbit around Teltos and hoped that the gravity was low enough and the atmosphere thin enough to stop him burning up. He had been proved right and the pod had come down close to the ruins of a derelict town. To his surprise and relief Shiro had found that though the Teltos air was thin, it was still adequate, and he had walked into the ruined streets of the town, certain somehow that eyes were watching him from doorways and crumbling arches.

It had been evening, already dark, when he first saw them. They had been crouched on their soft hindquarters in one of the town's ruined squares, staring through round, still eyes at the flickering light of the fire that they surrounded. They were chewing on strands of some plant root and they had been muttering to one another in a language that Shiro could not understand.

One of them had turned to face him as he approached their circle and Shiro, when he saw the dirt-flecked face that looked at him, had been startled. Perhaps it or its ancestors had once been human, but Shiro doubted it. As he stared at the broken teeth, the flat fore-head and slack jowls and the pointed canine ears, he was certain of one thing only: that evolution had ended for these creatures, that they were a species in the progress of de-generation. Yet he might be forced to spend the rest of his life here, he had thought, and he had found himself struggling against a sense of revulsion inside himself

as the creature beckoned him with large, spoonlike hands to sit down.

The creature spoke in a low grumbling moan to Shiro, words that he could not understand. They gathered around and peered at him, tugged and pinched at him, thrust their blank beasts' faces close to his, and laughed amongst themselves. When they did so Shiro had not-iced the sharpness of the jagged broken teeth in their jaws. He was given a rudely carved wooden bowl of liquid and leaves and some of the root they had been chewing. The liquid tasted sweet, like honey, and the leaves and root tasted bitter.

Soon his head had begun to feel heavy and his senses full of a dull warmth, and the flickering light from the fire had cast a slow, hypnotic spell upon him. He had watched the flames rise and the fire die as if he were watching the passage of a life, and he noticed with some dim part of his brain that was still aware that the creatures were dancing and chanting around him, as if he were at the centre of some ritual. His eyes wouldn't close and his limbs wouldn't move, and as he sat and gazed at the embers he didn't notice the strange creatures who had greeted him slipping silently away.

He had been alone in the square when he was woken by the sound of a spacecraft overhead. Daylight had been breaking. It had been an Alliance craft and it had been piloted by Makara. Her amplified voice had echoed round the empty square. "Good morning, Hagen. How did you enjoy the last night of your life? I see you have already met my hunters. Did they share their food and drink with you? It is a ritual they perform before every hunt and sacrifice."

"How did you know I'd be here, Makara?" Shiro had shouted over the sound of the engines.

"Simple, Hagen; you had only enough oxygen for one day, where else could you go? I knew you would come here. These creatures are already in the power of the Alliance. They regard the Imperial Master as a god. He has promised them a sacrifice, and with it his power here will be absolute. He has promised them your bones, Hagen! We shall hunt you down today."

Shiro shivered at the memory as he crouched in the cave, and then his thoughts snapped back to the present as the creatures emerged from the second cave and he watched Makara drive them further up the slope with her whip. They were moving on all fours across the boulders now, snarling and snapping at one another like animals eager for the kill. In his hiding place Shiro tensed himself and waited for the attack that he knew must come soon, and as he did so his mind raced back across the nightmarish events of that morning.

He remembered how Makara had told him to run and he had run. How the creatures had pursued him through the alleys and ruined buildings of the town. How he had hidden, breathless in the thin Teltos air, beneath an iron bridge, and how as he stood there he had felt the soft flat fingertips of one of the creatures at his throat. He remembered how they had struggled, how the creature's grip had tightened and how the sharp broken teeth had snapped in front of his face, and how he had taken a jagged black stone from the bed of the dry river and brought it down on the creature's skull. Behind him he had heard the strange whoops and howling cries of the creature's companions as they had scoured the ruined town for him.

Shiro had followed the dry river bed up into the hills and black rocks that lay behind the town, climbing upward, tumbling over boulders and scrambling across ravines until he had reached the high peak, and there he had hidden in the cave. And he had watched them come inexorably after him, moving in a ragged line

over the black boulders towards him.

Makara had been calling taunts to him, telling him that it was no use hiding, that there could be no escape from his fate. "I have promised you to them," she had shrieked. "You are their sacrifice."

And now, thought Shiro as he watched the creatures scrabble over the black rocks towards him, their eyes no longer soft and opaque but narrow and fired by some terrible hunger . . . now the moment was here. They had found him.

He stood up. If he had to die

then he would die fighting and not hidden in a cave. "Over here, Makara," he called out defiantly and watched them turn toward him, babbling and scratching as they clawed their way over the last few boulders to reach him.

And then suddenly the hunters had turned and were fleeing past Makara, down over the boulders and back towards the ruined town.

"Liars," Makara was shrieking, "Star Fleet liars." And she tried to stop the hunters' desertion with her whip. "You lied to me, Hagen. You and your crew gave your

word that you would be left here alone. Star Fleet liars!"

A giant shadow was suddenly cast across them both and Shiro turned to see the reason why Makara was cursing and the hunters had run. Looming up over the peak from its far slope was the giant figure of Dai-X.

From Brainder's loudhailers Shiro heard the sound of Doctor Benn's amplified voice call out. "Not me, Makara. I wasn't there, remember? I was on board your carrier. With another Makara and another Hagen. And neither of them promised anything either. I promised you nothing, but now, unless you want to die, you will promise me something."

"What do you want, you cowards?" shrieked Makara.

"That you and the Alliance leave this place and its poor creatures alone. They have suffered enough since the devastation."

Shiro watched Makara's face contort with hatred. She did not reply, and Doctor Benn's voice echoed over the hillside again. "Promise, Makara, or you die."

"Very well then, you have my word," said Makara, her features still defiant in defeat.

"All right, Makara, you can go this time," said Doctor Benn, and Shiro watched as she turned away and hurried down the slope with her cape trailing out behind her.

Later, back on X-Bomber, he asked Doctor Benn whether he thought Makara would keep her promise.

"No," said Doctor Benn, "but we can only wait and see. Should the Imperial Alliance try to interfere with Teltos again they will find a Star Fleet garrison there to defend it. And now, PPA, chart out the quickest course back to Earth — it seems a long while since we were there."

"You better do as he says, and quick," said Shiro, grinning. "Makara taught me one thing at least."

"And what was that?" asked PPA.

"How to deal with uppity little robots."

The Enemy

The enormous and powerful
Imperial Alliance space carrier,
commanded by Captain Orion,
with two of the Imperial fighters.

THE FORGOTTEN MEMORY

Shiro Hagen stood on the bridge of the Gelmar Force's carrier beside Makara and Captain Orion. Somewhere, out among the stars or lost within his memory, were a hidden question and an answer that eluded him.

"Do you understand your orders, Shiro Hagen?" asked Makara. Her black claw was clasped upon her sword handle and her harsh, hissing voice cut through Shiro's troubled thoughts.

"Yes, Makara, I am to return in Brainder to X-Bomber. Once I have docked I must deliver the X-Bomber into your hands."

"And what about its crew?"

"They are of no importance. My mission is only to bring back the X-Bomber intact. If they oppose me in this I shall kill them."

The unmasked half of Makara's face twisted with amusement. "And you have no doubts about your mission?"

"Doubts, Makara?" asked Shiro, puzzled by her question, "Why should I have doubts? Doubts are a weakness. Doctor Benn and the crew of X-Bomber have stood in the way of our Imperial Master for too long now. With the X-Bomber in Alliance hands then the Gelmar Force can breach the Thalian zone and seize the power which is rightfully our Imperial Master's and which Star Fleet has struggled so long to deny him."

"Excellent, Hagen. Remember, obedience to the Master is its own reward, we live only to serve him. Orion, take Hagen to his ship."

Brainder was docked in one of the carrier's huge fighter bays. It had been there, Shiro remembered, since his defection from X-Bomber. He thought of how he had told Doctor Benn that he was going to fly a routine patrol to investigate Alliance activity in quadrant ten; how he had left the quadrant at hyperspeeds and then, when he was certain that he was not being followed by any of the other Star Fleet fighters, he had sought out Makara and the Gelmar Force and offered her his services.

It had been the first wise move he had ever made in his life, he realised, as he checked Brainder's systems switches on the console in front of him. He heard Orion give him his departure clearance and watched the aperture in the carrier's side slide open to reveal the stars. If his mission was successful, thought Shiro, then it was only a matter of time before all these stars were under the control of the Imperial Master. And his mission was bound to be successful, for he lived only to serve the Imperial Master.

He flew the course that Makara had plotted for him, emerging into quantum space from hyperspeeds in quadrant ten. Locating X-Bomber didn't take long. It was just as Makara had predicted. Even now, eighteen days since his disappearance, they were still searching for him.

He shook his head in wonder and contempt. Eighteen days wasted in a search for a single crew member who, for all they knew, was probably dead. What weakness and what waste! Once the Power was in the hands of the Imperial Master then such weakness would be crushed. The universe would function in its most simple and efficient way. The rule of strength would prevail, just as it had prevailed before the great devastation. Doctor Benn and the other Star Fleet commanders all claimed peace as their goal, the rebuilding of what had been destroyed by the great devastation, but Shiro could see now what a pathetic and pitiful fallacy such hopes were based upon. They were deluded fools, the last remnants of an old order that had failed once before. Their way was not strong enough, they could not survive.

Suddenly the excited sound of Barry Hercules' voice was buzzing through his communicator. "Shiro, is that you? Come in, Shiro. Do you copy? Do you copy?"

"I copy, Barry," replied Shiro.

"Shiro, welcome home! What's been happening? Where have you been? We'd almost given you up. Thought you must have been downed by those Gelmar Force fighters."

"Check docking trajectories, Barry," said Shiro. "And switch your approach beam onto Brainder's locking co-ordinates. I'll explain it once I'm back aboard."

"Okay, Shiro, it sure is good to hear your voice again. Even PPA has missed you."

Once back on board the X-Bomber he was greeted with the same warmth and excitement that Barry had shown. As they gathered around him and embraced him and shook his hand and clapped him on the back, Shiro thought how pathetic they all were, slaves to the cowardly foolishness of friendship. It was a burden they refused to put down, a fault that prevented them using the X-Bomber for its natural, aggressive purpose. When he had delivered it to Makara, X-Bomber would be used in the way it should always have been used: to conquer.

"Oh, Shiro," said Lamia, her arms around his neck. She seemed overjoyed, almost on the verge of tears as she spoke. "When John Lee said that he'd lost your trace on his scanner screen then I began to worry. PPA calculated the probabilities and said that you must be dead, but I never believed him."

"That's right," said Fatty Lee, "when we lost sight of you on the edge of the quadrant you were spinning out of control. It seemed most likely that Alliance fighters had got you, but we never gave up hope. Doctor Benn has had us flying search patterns for the last eighteen days."

"It wasn't necessary," said Shiro flatly. "Just a failure in the support systems. Engines, communications, navigations and weapons all went dead. I couldn't contact you and I couldn't get back."

"How did you manage to fix them? There isn't the technology aboard Brainder to carry out major repairs," said Hercules, and Shiro looked at the smiling faces that surrounded him. Were they becoming suspicious behind their smiles or was the question prompted by their simple, innocent curiosity, another example of the pathetic concern that they seemed to feel for a lost colleague?

No matter, he had learned from Makara how dangerous their curiosity could be, how it undermined obedience to the Imperial Master. They had asked the question and sealed their own fate in asking it.

He could no longer take the risk of letting them live. It would have to be Doctor Benn first, he thought, and after telling Hercules that it had only been a chance

stroke of fortune that the crew of a passing supply freighter had spotted him and come to his rescue and Brainder's repair, he turned and spoke to the commander of X-Bomber and told him that he needed to speak to him.

"Then speak, Shiro," said Doctor Benn, smiling.

"Alone," said Shiro. "And it must be soon."

The commander of the X-Bomber frowned and asked Shiro why it was so important that they were alone when he made his report.

"You will see why when I tell you, sir," said Shiro impatiently.

"Very well then, Shiro," said Doctor Benn. "Be on the control deck in twenty minutes. That gives you enough time to take the data from Brainder's memory banks that PPA will need to make an analysis of your report."

"Very well, sir. In twenty minutes I shall be there," said Shiro.

When he arrived on the control deck he had already decided what he would do. He would shoot Doctor Benn with his laser pistol and then call for the others to come up. When they arrived he would shoot *them*.

Doctor Benn smiled at him when he came in and told him once again how worried they had all been by his absence.

"Worry is a failing, Doctor Benn. It makes people weak," said Shiro scornfully. "Star Fleet is weak and can never hope to defeat the might of the Imperial Master." Shiro drew his pistol as he spoke and held it at his old commander's head. "It is because of such weakness, the weakness of friendship, pity and concern, and the trust that you put in these pitifully fallible qualities, that you will die, Doctor Benn, and Star Fleet shall be defeated."

Shiro began to squeeze the trigger of the gun . . . but moments before the killing laser light was

released Barry Hercules had hurled himself from somewhere behind Shiro and sent them both tumbling to the ground.

Both men watched the gun slide across the floor of the control deck and they reached for it together. Shiro got there first. He heard Lamia shouting something and saw Fatty Lee with a pistol in his hand. If he was going to die in the service of the Master then he would take Star Fleet's top bomber crew with him.

But he felt Hercules' hand grab the gun once more and he saw Doctor Benn out of the corner of his eye approaching him with a tranquiliser jet.

And then everything went black.

When Shiro came to he was lying on an operating table in X-Bomber's medical bay. The tranquiliser had left his limbs feeling heavy, but when he tried to move them he discovered that he had been fastened to the table with tight straps.

Across the other side of the room he could see Lamia. She seemed to be pleading with Doctor Benn about something. Doctor Benn listened intently and

then gave a firm, sad shake of his head. He walked towards Shiro, pushing a machine in front of him. The machine contained a dish like a radar scanner and at its centre was a large, forked antenna. Lamia had hold of the Doctor's arm as he lowered and adjusted this device until the antenna were in contact with Shiro's forehead, and she was still pleading with him as he threw the switch.

Shiro felt a sudden bolt of pain shoot across his mind like a shuttle crossing a loom, and then there were lights flashing in front of him and everything around him seemed to be spinning. Gradually the spinning slowed to a point where he could recognise his surroundings.

He was back in Brainder's pilot seat and the flashing lights were the emergency signals on the

fighter's console warning him of severe malfunction. The spinning had been caused by the ship tumbling uncontrollably through the outer atmosphere of a planet as it fell towards its surface. Shiro wrestled desperately with the controls but it was no use, the fighter would no longer respond. Brainder was through the cloud level now and the planet's surface was visible, a flat, jungle land, threaded by meandering silver rivers. He searched for mountains or open plains, for oceans or some sign of habitation, but saw only the flat, endless forest and the sluggish silver rivers flowing nowhere, and it was into one of these that Shiro's fighter plunged, leaving a cascade of spray raining down onto the river's ruffled silver surface as it sank deeper and deeper through the water before coming to rest in the soft black mud of the riverbed.

Shiro was still checking Brainder's support systems for crash damage when there was a sudden heavy jolt on the outside of the ship and it tilted over in the mud. He glanced out of the observation window and saw sliding over the ancient black mud long-beaked, eyeless white creatures, their skins scaled and wax-soft, long tentacles with claws on the ends snapping blindly at Brainder as they approached.

Shiro watched them come out of the darkness. One, two, then two more, then four, then another three. There were too many of them. He scrambled into the life pod, hoping that it hadn't been damaged in the crash. His only hope was to abandon Brainder and take his chances on the surface.

He pulled the release switch and within seconds the lifepod had broken the surface and was bobbing in silver water beneath a silver sky. He pulled back the pod's canopy and scanned both shorelines. The closer of them was a mile away and from this distance seemed an unbroken

platform on stilts. Once again the message repeated in Shiro's head: GET READY.

A net shot down from the platform and enveloped him. He felt its ends sink and then close beneath him and suddenly he was being hoisted from the water. Aboard the platform the creatures gathered around him and helped him free of the net.

He looked at his rescuers. Their skins were the same pale silver as the river and the sky. They had smooth oval heads, without ears, nose, or mouth, the uniformity of their surface broken only by the two bulbous grey eyes set in each of them.

WELCOME. WE SAW YOUR CRAFT LAND.

Shiro grasped the six-fingered hand extended towards him and said, "I'm glad that you did. Those things would have killed me."

THEY ARE THE RIVER DWELLERS. WE KNOW THEM AS THE EATERS. TO THEM WE ARE KNOWN AS THE GATHERERS.

Shiro noticed that the platform had approached the closer of the two shores. From this distance he could see that what had appeared from further away to be an unbroken wall of trees and foliage was in fact a network of ramps, stairways, platforms, passageways and hanging tunnels, all suspended at different levels between the tree trunks.

When the craft had halted against one of the ramps, Shiro followed the silent silver creatures who called themselves the Gatherers into the maze of ramps and alleys that were suspended between an inhospitable, steaming marsh beneath and a luminous green roof of leaves and branches above.

They seemed to walk miles through this maze, passing groups of these creatures busy at tasks that Shiro could not understand; some pulling smooth white spheres from the water's edge, some spinning a fine silver thread from their fingertips, some carrying smooth-sided cocoons which they were placing in long tubular

wall of trees. Suddenly the pod was struck from underneath and cartwheeled up into the air. Shiro was flung clear as it struck the water again and sank. Tentacled claws were breaking the surface of the water all around him, opening and snapping closed like giant steel traps, snapping through one another's tentacles and sometimes their own, turning the churning water a blue green colour with their blood as they

sought blindly for their prey.

OVER HERE. GET READY. Shiro looked around in surprise. No one had called to him, and yet the message had arrived in his head and he had known exactly where it had come from. Walking through the river towards him, piloted by pale, smooth-skinned humanoids who seemed oblivious to the flailing tentacles and snapping claws that surrounded them, was a large mechanical

racks that had been cut into the sides of the broad tree trunks. Shiro asked what they were doing.

The reply entered his mind as he followed behind them. IT IS SIMPLY OUR WORK. THE REASON FOR OUR EXISTENCE. WE GATHER THE EGGS FROM THE WATER'S EDGE AND IT IS FROM THESE EGGS THAT WE OURSELVES ARE HATCHED. WHEN WE ENTER THE LONG SLEEP OUR BODIES ARE WRAPPED IN COCOONS AND STORED IN THESE RACKS. EVENTUALLY MUTATION OCCURS AND WE EMERGE TRANSFORMED. LOOK FOR YOURSELF. THEY ARE KNOWN TO US AS AIR DWELLERS.

They had emerged over a large still lake. All around it were flying, silver-winged creatures, similar to the Gatherers but with their bodies shrunken and tiny, their heads grown pale and bulbous, and their arms and legs grown long and thin as an insect's.

WITH THE AIR DWELLERS THE CHAIN IS COMPLETE. LIKE THE GATHERERS THEY HAVE THEIR PURPOSE; THOUGH UNLIKE THE GATHERERS IT IS ONE THAT THEY ARE UNABLE TO UNDERSTAND. THEY SEEK TO FLY UPWARD ALWAYS BUT EVENTUALLY THEY TIRE AND FALL TO THE WATER WHERE THEY ARE TAKEN BY THE EATERS. IT IS THE EATERS THAT LAY THE EGGS THAT WE GATHER FROM THE WATER'S EDGE. BUT YOU MUST SLEEP NOW, STRANGER, AND WHEN YOU HAVE SLEPT WE SHALL DECIDE WHAT MUST BE DONE TO HELP YOU.

Shiro, as if hypnotised, was unable to resist. When he awoke a group of Gatherers were pushing his body into one of the racks alongside a cocoon. When Shiro asked what they were doing, they answered him with the same still, calm voice that he could hear only inside his head.

DO NOT BE ALARMED. THERE ARE OTHER STRANGERS HERE THAT SEEK YOU.

WE PLACE YOU HERE FOR YOUR SAFETY. PLEASE REMAIN.

But Shiro wouldn't remain, his curiosity was too great, and he climbed down from where the Gatherers had tried to hide him and followed behind them through the maze of tunnels and sudden vistas of silver water until in the distance he heard the sound of a voice that he recognised.

It was Makara's voice and she was calling out, "Shiro Hagen, you are trapped. We already have your ship. Give yourself up or these creatures shall die."

Shiro emerged behind the Gatherers at the edge of one of the rivers. On one of the stilt platforms were Makara and a squad of her fiercest clone troopers. They held another group of Gatherers prisoner there, and Makara was throwing them one by one to the snapping claws of the Eaters.

"Hagen," shouted Makara again, "give yourself up before more die."

And then the Gatherers spoke silently to him again: DO NOT GIVE YOURSELF UP, SHIRO HAGEN. WE COME FROM THE RIVERS AND WE RETURN TO THEM. THIS CREATURE CAN DO US NO HARM.

Shiro hesitated. There was truth in what they said. Yet they

had saved him from the claws of the Eaters. As he looked at the broken limbs of these peaceful creatures that died in such eerie silence in the foaming, blood stained water he knew he could not remain silent.

After he had shouted to them Makara's clones acted quickly. They took Shiro up to the orbiting Gelmar carrier on a shuttle. There he was clamped into a chair with a black metal hood above it. After a while Makara came in and asked him if he was comfortable.

"Why don't you just kill me, Makara?" asked Shiro defiantly.

"I have a much better use for you alive, Hagen. But first I am going to steal your memory." With a hissing laugh Makara lowered the metal hood over Shiro's face and all of his thoughts disintegrated into burning white light.

When Shiro opened his eyes again he was lying on the table in X-Bomber's medical bay and the bomber's smiling crew were all gathered around him. He pressed his fingers to his head; he could not remember what had happened to him.

Doctor Benn explained as simply as he could. "You crashed and were captured by Makara. She put you underneath a memory destructor, then gave you a false memory and sent you back here to kill us and take over X-Bomber. I suspected that there was something wrong; that's why John and Barry were waiting on the control deck. Once we had overpowered you we had to reverse the polarities of Makara's implants. It was risky, but we had no other choice. We watched the whole thing on the screen of the neuro-processor."

"That's right," said John Lee. "The dog fight over the planet . . . your crash landing in the river . . . the attack by the Eaters . . ."

"You mean all that wasn't just a dream?"

"No, Shiro. That was the memory that Makara had stolen from you. Only by giving it back to you could we destroy the false memory that she'd left you with."

"I tried to kill you." Shiro couldn't bear to look at his friends as he spoke.

"No, Shiro," said Lamia, and put her hand upon his shoulder. "That was just a monster that Makara created. The real Shiro Hagen was the man who gave himself up rather than permit Makara to kill any more of the Gatherers."

"Correct, Lamia," intoned PPA beside them, "the real Shiro Hagen. His action was impulsive, thoughtless, illogical and un necessary. The Gatherers had already informed him of their indestructibility."

"Maybe, bubblebrain," said Barry Hercules, "but what if they were wrong?"

"One moment," said PPA, the transparent top of his dome revolving and lights flashing on and off inside him. "It is necessary to re-analyse the data in light of new possibilites. Since first premise of Eaters' society must be . . ."

But everything was back to normal on X-Bomber. No one was listening to him.

The Final Test

How much do you know about Star Fleet? Are you ready to take the Final Test? If you think you're prepared, then go ahead — but remember, protect yourself. Those who know too much are always in danger from Makara and the Imperial Alliance . . .

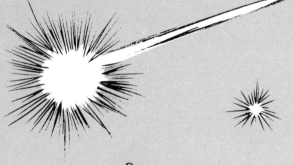

1. What is the Thalian Zone?
2. Which planet is the leader of the Solar System?
3. Who is in charge of the Earth's defence force?
4. Which planet was Lamia found on?

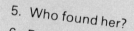

5. Who found her?
6. Doctor Benn would prefer his spaceship used for what purpose?
7. What does PPA stand for?
8. What is the aim of the Imperial Alliance?

9. Who is the commanding officer of the Alliance's huge space carrier?
10. What is the name of the huge robot piloted by Shiro, Barry and John?
11. Which of them pilots the head of the robot?
12. Which of them pilots the feet and legs of the robot?

13. Which of them controls the body of the robot?

14. X-Bomber has a very powerful, last-resort weapon which consumes huge amounts of energy. Can you name it?

15. How many times can this particular weapon be used in a confrontation?

16. What is the name of Lamia's fierce alien bodyguard?

17. Who is in command of the Imperial Alliance's forces?

18. This person has to answer to only one other. Who is he?

19. Where is X-Bomber's base?

20. Who began the work on X-Bomber, and who completed that work?

PANIC on the Graveyard Run

John Lee was puzzled by the message he had just received. It was faint, its origin was unknown, and it didn't make any sense. He ran it through the decoding computer.

"What have you got, John?" asked Barry Hercules, leaning over his shoulder.

"Trouble," replied John, "we'd better get Doctor Benn."

Doctor Benn studied the decoded message with a frown.

"There's an outbreak of Zukonic Plague on the Ekstar Observation Base," he explained. "They need more Stubby Juice."

"The plague vaccine?" asked Shiro.

Doctor Benn nodded. "Without it, they'll die. We're going to have to make the Graveyard Run."

The crew of X-Bomber fell silent. They had all heard of the Graveyard Run, but only Doctor Benn had made it. In fact, Doctor Benn was one of the very few living beings who'd come out of the Graveyard Run alive and sane.

The Graveyard Run was the name given to the spacewarp that surrounded the Ekstar base. Veteran pilots told of the strange beings that lurked there: of mysterious planetoids, vapours and radioactive emissions. They told how the instruments on their ships had malfunctioned, how engines had started up of their own accord, how lights had gone on and off, hatches had blown from their hinges. When pressed, a few would mention the 'aura of evil' that filled the zone.

"Can't we just warp through?" asked Shiro.

"Negative," said Doctor Benn. "It's too dangerous. We'll have to go through it at Quantum speed. If we tried to warp through we might end up in another galaxy one hundred years into the future."

They flew back to Saturn Base to pick up the Stubby Juice, and then began preparations for their mission.

"We'll go into hyperspeed here," said Doctor Benn, pointing to an electronic chart. "And we'll warp out there, on the edge of the spacewarp."

"Let's get this show on the road then," said Shiro, steering the huge X-Bomber to the jump-off point.

"I'm afraid I must point out the dangerous nature of this mission," said PPA. "It's all right to go dashing off risking your lives, but my job is to safeguard this ship — oh, oh!" PPA scuttled under the storage hold as Barry Hercules aimed a tungsten steel diamond-tipped hammer drill at him.

"All systems ready?" asked Shiro.

"Ready," confirmed Barry Hercules.

"Just a minute!" interrupted John Lee. "Unidentified craft — M12 and closing!"

"Alliance starfighters!" said Shiro. "Hold on — I'm taking evasive action!"

"No!" said Doctor Benn. "Warp to hyperspeed!"

Shiro didn't hesitate in setting the controls as John Lee charted the path of the oncoming enemy fighters.

"7 . . . 5 . . . 3 . . . they'll be opening fire any second," he warned.

"Going into hyperspeed," said Shiro calmly, as the Alliance fighters opened up with their Beam Guns.

Suddenly X-Bomber shuddered violently. There was a rush of colour and sound, and then a flash of light signalled their entry into hyperspace.

"Any damage?" asked Shiro.

"Sensors indicate a slight crack by the caterpillars in Legstar. Sealants activated."

As they settled down to await their arrival on the edge of the Graveyard Run, Doctor Benn pondered the reasons for the Alliance attack. Without battle cruiser back-up, the fighters could hardly have hoped to eliminate X-Bomber. But the scanners had indicated that no battle cruiser was in that quadrant of space. Of course, it could have been a nuisance strike, a hit-and-run attack, but . . .

"Ready to decelerate," said Shiro, cutting into Doctor Benn's thoughts.

"Proceed!" said Doctor Benn. "The rest of you — take up action stations."

Doctor Benn's caution proved justified. Fighter spaceships such as X-Bomber were always at their most vulnerable when entering or leaving hyperspace, when both crew and instruments needed a few vital seconds to re-adjust their bearings. This time, as the flash of colours gave way to the blackness of quantum speed space, they saw the menacing form of the Gelmar Force battle cruiser waiting at their re-entry point.

X-Bomber was rocked as the battle cruiser opened fire, pumping high-powered laser pulses into its defenceless hull.

"Shields up!" commanded Shiro. "Battle stations!"

Shiro flung X-Bomber into immediate action. They zoomed first forwards, then up, then to the right and then the left.

"Brest Cannon ready?" he asked Doctor Benn.

"Ready."

Under Shiro's expert guidance X-Bomber went into a steep dive followed by a tight loop that gave Doctor Benn an excellent view of the Gelmar Force battle cruiser's underbelly.

As the huge, quick-firing laser beam wreaked havoc with the battle cruiser's defences, Commander Makara turned angrily to Captain Orion.

"You fool!" she snarled. "You've wasted the perfect chance to wipe out Doctor Benn and his cowardly crew. What's the use of us tapping their communication system if you can't make good use of the information we receive?"

"But, Commander —"

"Silence! We must fight!"

The battle raged throughout the quadrant, with no quarter asked and none given. The X-Bomber's greater manoeuvrability meant that it was hit less often, but the battle cruiser's stronger defences were proving extremely difficult to break down completely. So fierce was the fighting that neither Makara nor Shiro noticed that both ships had entered the Graveyard Run.

It was Barry Hercules who first noticed there was something wrong.

"Malfunction in right X-Machine Gun!" he warned.

Kirara began jumping up and down and Lamia shivered nervously.

"Battle cruiser moving out of

range," said John Lee.

PPA began floating in the air emitting steam from his upper ducts.

"Alien aboard! Alien aboard!" he shrieked.

"What?" asked Lamia.

"My sensors indicate that there is an alien presence on board X-Bomber," PPA said.

"Take no notice of him," said Barry Hercules. "Doctor Benn has already told us how machines malfunction on the Graveyard Run."

"That's right," agreed Doctor Benn. "We must stick to the course I mapped out previously. We must ignore all electronic readings."

A scream from Lamia brought them to her side. She was staring out of a vid-lock and pointing into space. There, less than twenty feet away, writhing and foaming from its gaping mouth, its long yellow claws sunk deep into the horns of its adversary, a Space Serpent was fighting for its life against a gigantic flying Rhino-thon.

"Don't worry," said Doctor Benn soothingly. "They're too busy to bother with us. They don't —" His words were cut short when the whole ship was suddenly plunged into darkness.

"Get to your posts," ordered Shiro.

Their intimate knowledge of X-Bomber's interior helped the crew back to their positions.

"Manual control," said Doctor Benn, "exactly as planned."

"Copy!" said Shiro. "Is everybody all right?"

"I'm a little cold," said Lamia. "How about you, Hercules?"

There was no answer. Lamia shivered in the darkness.

"Hercules?" repeated Lamia. "Are you there?"

There was still no answer — only silence and blackness.

"Hercules? Shiro? Doctor Benn? Stop playing games!"

Lamia was getting nervous. Where were the others? She couldn't see anything in the darkness. It was as if she were totally alone — except for the uneasy feeling that someone — some

thing — was watching her.

"Kirara? PPA? Isn't anybody there?"

Lamia felt a prickly sensation at the back of her neck. Where were they? What had happened? They couldn't have just vanished. It was impossible. It didn't make sense.

And then Lamia's ears picked up a sound, so faint that at first she thought she had imagined it, but growing louder and louder every second. It came from somewhere behind her, the sound of breathing, long low rasping breaths that were coming closer and closer towards her. The sudden smell of sulphur filled her nostrils and when she felt the scaly reptilian fingers on her shoulders she screamed and leapt to her feet.

Lamia lashed out with her fists as she tried to push the creature away. Her hands touched something cold and slimy and through the blackness she imagined she could see the glint of long yellow teeth and small shiny red eyes.

"Doctor Benn! Help! Kirara!" cried Lamia.

But the only answer was silence . . . and the angry breathing of the intruder. She backed away from the sound and then turned and ran towards Doctor Benn's command post.

"Doctor Benn! Please help me!"

In the twinkling light of a single, distant star, Lamia could see a figure seated at the controls.

"Doctor Benn?"

Lamia inched nervously forward and the chair swung suddenly round. The sight that greeted her was not the kindly features of Doctor Benn, however, it was the hideous, mocking grin of a human skeleton. Lamia was about to scream when she felt the cold grip of alien hands tightening round her throat.

"Lamia! Wake up! What's the matter?"

Suddenly X-Bomber was flooded with light and Lamia found herself staring into the warm, concerned gaze of Shiro and Hercules.

"Lamia! Are you all right?" asked Shiro, shaking her. "Lamia, wake up! It's over! We've done it! We've made the Graveyard Run!"

"But — but —" Lamia looked dazed.

Doctor Benn put a hand gently on her shoulder. "It's quite an experience isn't it?" he said reassuringly. "The secret is to ignore whatever you think is happening to you."

"And it's not easy," said John Lee, "when you're absolutely con-vinced you've turned into a six-foot space slug."

"Is that what you thought?" asked Hercules. "I imagined that X-Bomber had caught fire and I was face to face with an Occamese Kangabat."

"That doesn't sound too bad," said John Lee.

"It is when you think you're only two inches high," replied Hercules. "How Shiro kept us on course, I'll never know."

"I just followed Doctor Benn's instructions," explained Shiro, "and stuck to our pre-arranged course — even when my instruments told me I was flying backwards at hyperspeed into a black hole."

"Didn't you see any monsters at

all?" asked Lamia.

"Well —" began Shiro. PPA inspected the floor by Shiro's seat.

"What are these marks?" he asked. "And why are your shoes scratched?"

Shiro shrugged. "Well — I'd known what to expect, but I couldn't help it. There were so many of them, crawling all over the floor."

"Snakes?" asked John Lee.

Shiro shook his head. "Spiders," he explained. "Radio-active ones that sprayed acid. Even though I knew they weren't real I was still terrified."

"We all were," said Doctor Benn. "The Graveyard Run has claimed many victims."

"What did you imagine, Doctor?" Lamia asked.

"Yes, Doctor, what did you think was happening?"

The crew of X-Bomber crowded round Doctor Benn eagerly.

"Well, first of all," said Doctor Benn with a smile, "I imagined that X-Bomber was flooded with green liquid and that I had developed gills and a large fin. And then I found I was strapped in my seat, but I had no hands to unfasten myself. I was caught fast and a shoal of tiny fish with razor sharp teeth were taking bites out of me."

"That's awful," said Lamia.

"That's the Graveyard Run," said Doctor Benn. "Now let's get this vaccine down to Ekstar at once."

Shiro set the controls for the descent onto Ekstar.

"Doctor Benn?" he asked. "Do you think Makara and Orion made it?"

"I don't know," said Doctor Benn. "With any luck they're still stuck in there."

"Let's hope they stay that way," said Hercules, "trapped in a nightmare of their own imaginings."

"And from what we know about them in the real world," added Shiro, "that's one mean nightmare."

The crew of X-Bomber smiled grimly as they came in to land.

THE OBSERVATION GAME

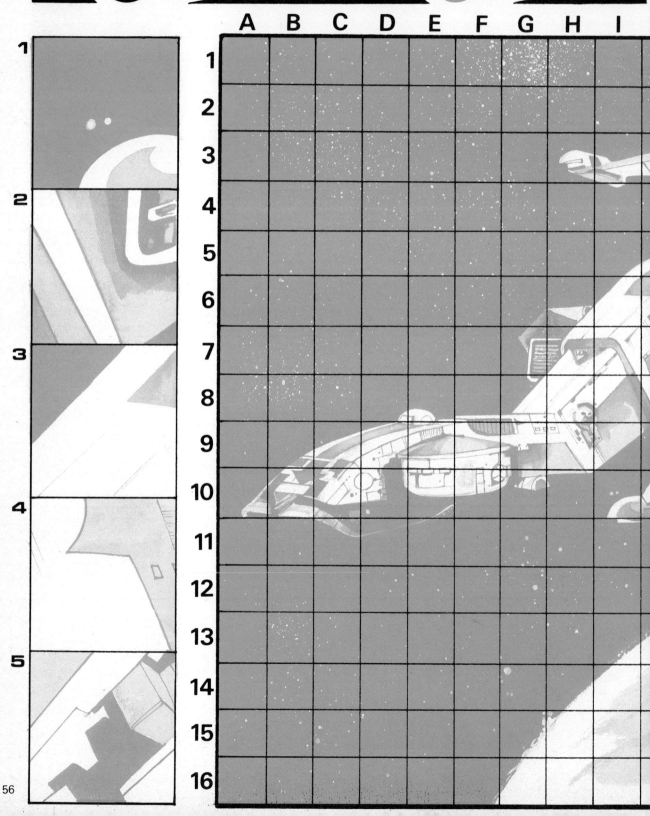

You have to be sharp of eye to be a space pilot with Star Fleet. How observant are *you*? Here you can see a view of the X-Bomber as it sets off on another mission to do battle against the evil Commander Makara. You must study this very carefully, and then look at the ten enlarged sections of the picture. Can you tell where these sections have been taken from?

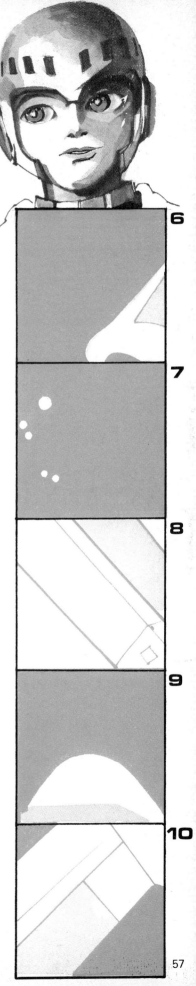

The MUTANT WORM attack

It began with an urgent distress call from the Intersolar Mining Company on the planet SWX 3. The message was simple: "Come quickly — we're under attack!"

X-Bomber was on a routine flight round the outer defences of the Saturn base when the call came through.

"What do you think, Doctor Benn?" asked Shiro.

Doctor Benn swivelled round in his seat.

"We go," he said simply.

"But SWX 3 is in the Jarrad Sector," protested Barry Hercules. "Surely we can't afford to —"

"We go," repeated Doctor Benn.

"You're the boss," said Shiro, and while PPA began computing their course, he began preparing the powerful X-Bomber engines for the leap between quantum and hyperspeed.

"It's no good!" shrilled PPA. "It's 12 Militons to SWX 3. By the time we arrive any fighting will be over."

"We go," said Doctor Benn.

Shiro noticed the depth of commitment in his voice and set X-Bomber on its voyage.

In fact, PPA was wrong. When X-Bomber arrived at SWX 3, a fearful battle was raging. The Alliance battle cruiser, in the charge of Commander Makara and Captain Orion, was standing guard as carriers ferried more Alliance Imperial Fighters to join the ones already engaged in attacking the smoking dome on the rocky surface of SWX 3.

Not that the Alliance were having it all their own way. A barrage of Lazooka and Magnetic Cannon fire from the dome ripped defiantly through the attacking Imperial Fighters.

"Take the Dai-X, Shiro," said Doctor Benn. "I'll take on the battle cruiser."

Shiro, Barry Hercules and John Lee acted quickly. With Shiro at the controls, Brainder disengaged from the X-Bomber, soon to be followed by Barry Hercules in Jumbody and John Lee in Legstar.

"Barry," said Shiro into his communicator, "you and I will go for the astro fighters. John — you go down to the mining base and give them ground support."

"We copy," said John Lee, adjusting Legstar's controls and swooping low towards the planet base.

As Shiro and Barry Hercules threw Brainder and Jumbody into the thick of the action, Doctor Benn was also hard at work, setting the controls to lift the X-Bomber's nose and reveal the huge Brest Cannon underneath. He swung X-Bomber round in a tight turn and began bearing down on the well fortified Alliance battle cruiser.

On board that same battle cruiser, Commander Makara and Captain Orion were seething with anger at the arrival of their long-hated enemy.

"Commander, the battle is turning," said Orion, staring at a screen that showed Jumbody and Brainder wreaking havoc among his own fighters. "Perhaps it would be prudent —"

He was cut short by a tremendous explosion that rocked the battle cruiser from side to side and sent him and Commander Makara crashing against the control panels.

"What was that?" snarled Makara.

"It's X-Bomber," replied Orion. "It's attacking us with its quickfire Laser Brest Cannon. We must call back the fighters at once!"

Another blast from the X-Bomber shook the cruiser as Doctor Benn came in close.

"Curse that Doctor Benn!" spat Makara. "Orion — order the retreat! This time we were unready. But I swear by our Imperial Master that X-Bomber will feel the full force of the revenge of our Imperial Alliance!"

"Looks like they're on the run, Shiro," said Barry Hercules as he put Jumbody through a rolling curve to avoid the exploding debris of the last Imperial Fighter he had hit with his Beam Gun.

"Sure does, Barry," said Shiro as he watched the fighters link up with their carriers and turn back for the relative safety of the Gelmar Force cruiser.

Doctor Benn's voice came crackling over the communicators. "That's enough, Shiro," he said. "Break off and return to X-Bomber. We're going in to land."

"I copy," said Shiro.

Shiro and Hercules returned Brainder and Jumbody to X-Bomber and Doctor Benn landed close to the dome. John Lee was standing beside Legstar talking to a tall, thin man dressed in white.

"Glad you could make it," said the man as the crew of X-Bomber disembarked. "My name's Soltar, the elected leader of this outpost. The air's not all it might be out here, but I think you'll find it more pleasant inside."

Soltar was right. Outside the dome, the air was heavy and dusty with a strong smell of decay. Inside the dome it was light and fragrant. Soltar led them into a low white building that was filled with mineral evaluation equipment.

"This is where we check the ore," said Soltar.

"Very impressive," said Doctor Benn. "Have you any samples from your moon?"

"Yes, we've just begun preliminary excavations there." Soltar activated a screen that glowed with coloured graphs and numbers.

"Hmm," said Doctor Benn, "this analysis would indicate an uncommonly high level of radiation."

"I know," said Soltar, "and the worrying thing is – it's getting worse."

Doctor Benn checked the figures on the screen yet again.

"Is anything wrong?" asked Soltar.

"I'm afraid so," said Doctor Benn. "There's something very wrong indeed. How long would it take you to evacuate the entire base?"

"Hey, just a minute! Just what are you talking about?"

Doctor Benn wiped his forehead with the back of his hand.

"A long time ago," he began, "before the war, planet SWX 3 was known as Steene. Before the population was wiped out Steene had an enviable reputation as a peaceful, progressive civilisation. Ironically the peace of Steene rested heavily on the invention of the Z-Rad Multibomb."

"What do you mean?"

"The records are incomplete, but before the invention of the Z-Rad Multibomb, Steenians were an extremely warlike race, constantly fighting one another. The Z-Rad stopped all that."

"How?" asked Lamia.

Doctor Benn shrugged. "The power of the Z-Rad Multibomb was so great that anybody who used it would start an explosion that would destroy the whole planet. This knowledge led the Steenians into finding other ways of solving their differences. There was only one snag."

"What was that?" asked Soltar.

"Once the Steenians had built the bomb — they didn't know how to get rid of it. Their space programme was still in its infancy —"

"So they buried it on the moon," said Soltar.

"Exactly. We knew all of this from the bits of history that survived the war. The only thing we didn't know was where Steene was. Now we do."

"But surely if it's been there for thousands of years —" said Shiro.

Doctor Benn pointed to the screen. "It appears that the bomb has de-stabilised. The radiation it gives off is doubling all the time. If my calculations are correct, it's fast approaching a critical stage."

"What will happen?" asked John Lee.

"When the Z-Rad Multibomb detonates, the chain reaction will explode the moon," said PPA. "It will turn into a gigantic fireball approximately seventy-six point four times its present diameter. Temperatures on this planet would become so great that all living matter would be reduced to dust."

"Thanks a million, PPA," said

Hercules. "What do you suggest we do?"

"X-Bomber must leave immediately," said PPA, hovering up and down in an agitated manner. "We must warp out of this sector as soon as possible."

"But what about the people we leave behind?" asked Lamia.

"Insufficient data!" piped PPA. "Cannot compute! Insufficient data!"

Doctor Benn held up his hand for silence. "We're taking X-Bomber to the moon to find the bomb," he said. "And there will be no further discussion. Let's go."

They left Soltar at the dome and boarded X-Bomber. John Lee joined Legstar up with X-Bomber on the trip to the moon.

"Our records suggest the Steenians buried the bomb deep in one of their caves," said Doctor Benn as Shiro piloted X-Bomber over the rough surface of the moon. "And that our best point of entry would be at 14:24:17."

"I copy, Doctor Benn," said Shiro, feeding the co-ordinates into his computer. "Hold onto yourselves — we're going in."

Shiro put X-Bomber down by the edge of a huge crater, and by the time the grey dust had settled, the crew of X-Bomber were heading into a cave in the crater wall.

"We're on the right track!" said Doctor Benn, checking the instrumentation on his radiation suit. "Be careful not to puncture your suits."

But Doctor Benn's warning was suddenly forgotten when the walls of the cave erupted in action and the crew of X-Bomber found its way blocked by a wobbling, shivering, shaking mass of transparent flesh.

"Mutant worms!" yelled Shiro, taking aim. "The radiation must have got to them."

As the giant worm slithered forward, its circular mouth opening and closing to reveal layer upon layer of short sharp white teeth,

Shiro and Hercules opened fire. The worm emitted a high pitched whistling noise and slumped forward.

"Yech!" said Lamia, as she followed Shiro through the narrow gap between the worm's body and the side of the cave. "Let's hope we find that bomb soon."

They did. It was found buried in the wall of the cave and clearly marked with drawings of skulls. It was about the size of a large suitcase and it was encased in concrete. It was also beginning to glow.

"Be careful with that thing," said Doctor Benn. "It's approaching an extremely critical stage. We don't want to shake it up at all!"

Slowly, carefully, Shiro and Hercules carried the bomb back up the cave, past the still warm body of the worm, over the lip of the crater and into the hold of X-Bomber.

"Right," said Doctor Benn, as X-

Bomber's crew took up their positions. "So far so good. Take us out of orbit, Shiro."

Shiro set the controls for take-off and pressed the controls. X-Bomber did not respond. He repeated the procedure. No response.

"What's the matter, Shiro?" asked Doctor Benn.

"I don't know, Doctor Benn. I —"

"Worms!" yelled John Lee. "Worms in the engines! They're coming aboard!"

"Can we burn them out?" asked Shiro.

"No way," said John Lee. "They're blocking the tubes. You start those engines and this ship will go up like a fireball."

"Doctor Benn?" asked Shiro.

"Take a party back," said Doctor Benn. "Fight them as long as you can — and make sure you wear your insulation suits."

Shiro, Hercules and John Lee made their way to the engine room. There, squirming and slithering their way into X-Bomber through the reactor tubes, were more of the gigantic mutant worms.

"Open up!" ordered Shiro. "Full power."

The three men opened fire with their laser pistols. One worm, hideously wounded, began snapping at its fellow mutants. The floor was covered with a dark, sticky substance. Shiro, Hercules and John Lee kept firing. The worms kept on coming.

"Ready?" barked Doctor Benn over the communicator.

"Copy."

"NOW!"

In the control room, Doctor Benn threw a switch and the whole of X-Bomber glowed and crackled as close to one million volts of electricity surged through its massive body. The worms whistled, sizzled and then vanished. They'd been completely vapourised.

Shiro dashed back to his post and X-Bomber's engines roared into life.

"Where to?" he asked.

"The nearest jump-off point," replied Doctor Benn.

X-Bomber reached the jump-off point and warped into hyper speed.

"When?" asked Shiro.

"Now!" said Doctor Benn.

X-Bomber slowed down to quantum speed and jettisoned the X-Rad Multibomb.

The last thing they saw as they warped back to hyperspeed was the bomb — glowing white and shedding bits of its casing — on the verge of exploding.

"Nasty looking device," said Shiro as they settled in hyperspeed. "I should imagine a bomb like that could give you quite a shock."

"It would," agreed Hercules. "But not half as bad a shock as we gave those worms!"

And X-Bomber reverberated with the sound of the relieved laughter of its crew.

The Mysterious Zodiac

You may not have realised that the twelve signs of the Zodiac were all taken from certain patterns of stars, or *constellations*, which move around the night sky from month to month. Well, this is the case — the expression *star sign* gives you a clue, doesn't it? Well, let's have a closer look at the constellations which make up the Zodiac. Which sign do you belong to?

Scorpius, The Scorpion

24 October — 22 November

Capricornus, The Goat

22 December — 20 January

Sagittarius, The Archer

23 November — 21 December

Libra, The Scales

24 September — 23 October

Leo, The Lion

24 July — 23 August

Virgo, The Virgin

24 August — 23 September